FLAMINGO IS BRAVE

A book about feeling SCARED

Written by Sue Graves

Illustrated by Trevor Dunton

Franklin Watts®
An imprint of Scholastic Inc.

Flamingo was scared of lots of things.
He was scared of **spiders**.

He was scared of **the dark**.

He was scared of **loud noises**, too.

At school, Flamingo was scared of playing soccer. He was scared he might kick the soccer ball **the wrong way**.

Flamingo was scared of **reading out loud**
even though he was a really good reader!

Flamingo was scared of playing hide-and-seek at recess. He was worried he **might get lost**.

When Flamingo got scared, he hid his head under his wing. He shivered and shook, and his knees knocked together. Flamingo didn't like being scared. He wanted to **be brave**.

On Friday, Monkey had some **exciting news**. It was his birthday the next day, and everyone was invited for a sleepover in his backyard.

Everyone was excited. Everyone except Flamingo. He was scared. What if a **spider** got in the tent? What if it got **too dark**? What if they played hide-and-seek and he **got lost**? Flamingo was sad.

When Flamingo got home, he went to find
Grandpa. Flamingo told Grandpa he was scared.
He said he wished he could **be brave**.
Grandpa said when he felt scared he pulled his
shoulders back and lifted his chin up. He said he
took a **deep breath**, too.

Flamingo pulled his shoulders back and
lifted his chin up. He took a deep breath.
Flamingo felt **a little better**.

Grandpa said everyone got scared sometimes.
He said when he was a little bird he was
scared of swimming. Flamingo was
surprised. He **liked swimming** very much.
It was fun!

Grandpa said he thought the water **looked scary**. He said his friends helped him. He soon **loved swimming**.

Flamingo thought he could ask his friends to help him. Grandpa said that was a great idea.

Flamingo went to see his friends.

He told them he was scared.

He said he wanted to be brave.

His friends said they would **help him**.

The next day, it was Monkey's party. First the friends played hide-and-seek. Flamingo felt scared. Then he remembered what Grandpa had said. Flamingo pulled his shoulders back, lifted his chin up, and took a deep breath. He **felt better**.

Everyone played the game. Everyone had fun.
And Flamingo **didn't get lost** at all.

Soon it was time for bed. Suddenly a spider ran across Flamingo's sleeping bag.

But Monkey showed Flamingo how to catch
the spider in a glass.
Flamingo **wasn't scared at all**.

It got darker and darker. Flamingo was worried that it would get **too dark**. But Tiger lent him his flashlight, and the dark **wasn't scary at all**.

Everyone said Flamingo was being **very brave**.

Just then, the friends heard a strange noise.
Everyone thought it was a monster **and hid**!
But Flamingo pulled his shoulders back,
lifted his chin up, and took a deep breath.
He peeked outside the tent.

24

25

It wasn't a monster at all. It was Monkey's big toy tractor, and that wasn't scary at all. Everyone laughed and said Flamingo was **very brave**!

Flamingo was proud. He liked being brave.
It was much better than being scared!

A note about sharing this book

The **Behavior Matters** series has been developed to provide a starting point for further discussion on children's behavior both in relation to themselves and others. The series features animal characters reflecting typical behavior traits often seen in young children.

Flamingo Is Brave
This story looks at some of the typical things that may scare children and investigates strategies for overcoming fears.

How to use the book
The book is designed for adults to share with an individual child or a group of children, and as a starting point for discussion.

The book also provides visual support and repeated words and phrases to build reading confidence.

Before reading the story
Choose a time to read when you and the children are relaxed and have time to share the story.

Spend time looking at the illustrations and talk about what the book might be about before reading it together.

Encourage children to tackle new words by sounding them out.

After reading, talk about the book with the children:

- Encourage the children to retell the events of the story in chronological order.

- Talk about the things that scare the children. Point out that many of their fears are also experienced by others and are especially common among children. Invite the children to share their fears with the group.

- Talk about how fears can be overcome. Many children like to have a night-light on if they are scared of the dark. Others like to have a favorite toy to take to bed. Encourage the children to share their ideas for coping with fears. Take the opportunity to share your own childhood fears with the children and explain how you overcame them.

- Point out the strategies mentioned in the story. Grandpa got his friends to help and encourage him. He also shows Flamingo how to pull his shoulders back, lift his chin up, and take a deep breath. Invite the children to stand up and try those steps for themselves. How does it make them feel?

- As a class, invite the children to help you write a list of the things that scare them. Ask the children to suggest ways of overcoming each fear. Leave the list on display for future reference.

For Isabelle, William A, William G, George, Max, Emily, Leo, Caspar, Felix, Tabitha, Phoebe, and Harry —S.G.

Library of Congress Cataloging-in-Publication Data
Names: Graves, Sue, 1950– author. | Dunton, Trevor, illustrator.
Title: Flamingo is brave: a book about feeling scared/written by Sue Graves; illustrated by
   Trevor Dunton.
Description: First edition. | New York: Franklin Watts, an imprint of Scholastic Inc., 2021. |
   Series: Behavior matters | Audience: Ages 4–7. | Audience: Grades K–1. | Summary:
   Flamingo is scared of many things, such as spiders, the dark, and getting lost, but his
   grandfather shows him how to be brave, and Flamingo explains his fears to his friends so
   they can all be brave together.
Identifiers: LCCN 2021000570 (print) | LCCN 2021000571 (ebook) |
   ISBN 9781338758108 (library binding) | ISBN 9781338758122 (paperback) |
   ISBN 9781338758139 (ebook)
Subjects: LCSH: Fear—Juvenile fiction. | Courage—Juvenile fiction. | Friendship—Juvenile
   fiction. | Grandfathers—Juvenile fiction. | CYAC: Fear—Fiction. | Courage—Fiction. |
   Friendship—Fiction. | Grandfathers—Fiction. | Flamingos—Fiction. | Animals—Fiction.
Classification: LCC PZ7.G7754 Fl 2021 (print) | LCC PZ7.G7754 (ebook) | DDC [E]—dc23
LC record available at https://lccn.loc.gov/2021000570
LC ebook record available at https://lccn.loc.gov/2021000571

10 9 8 7 6 5 4 3 2 1   22 23 24 25 26 27

Printed in China
First edition, 2022